Rise Of The Snow Queen
Book One:
The Polar Bear King

G.W. Mullins

© 2018 by G.W. Mullins

All rights reserved. No part of this publication may be reproduced, distributed, or transmitted in any form or by any means, including photocopying, recording, or other electronic or mechanical methods, without the prior written permission of the publisher, except in the case of brief quotations embodied in critical reviews and certain other noncommercial uses permitted by copyright law.

ISBN: 978-1-64008-095-9

First Printing

This is a work of fiction. Names, characters, businesses, places, events and incidents are either the products of the author's imagination or used in a fictitious manner. Any resemblance to actual persons, living or dead, or actual events is purely coincidental.

Light Of The Moon Publishing has allowed this work to remain exactly as the author intended, verbatim, without editorial input.

Printed in the United States of America

For further information, on his writing, visit G.W. Mullins' web site at
http://gwmullins.wix.com/books

The Polar Bear King

Other titles available from G.W. Mullins include:
Daniel Awakens A Ghost Story Begins - A *From The Dead Of Night* Book Series Prequel
Daniel Is Waiting A Ghost Story – *From The Dead Of Night* Book One
Daniel Returns - *From The Dead Of Night* Book Two
Daniel's Fate *From The Dead Of Night* Book Four
Vengeance
Messages Form the Other Side Stories of the Dead, Their Communication, and Unfinished Business
The Native American Story Book Volume 1-5- Stories Of The American Indians For Children
Walking With Spirits Volumes 1-6 Native American Myths, Legends, And Folklore
The Native American Cookbook
Star People, Sky Gods And Other Tales of The Native American Indians
Cherokee A Collection of American Indian Legends, Stories And Fables
Rise Of The Snow Queen Book One - The Polar Bear King
Rise Of The Snow Queen Book Two – War Of The Witches
Animal Tales Of The Native American Indians
Jason And Alexander
Jason And Alexander The Return
Time After Time

Mullins

For Clarence

The Polar Bear King

The following book and the others included in this series are loosely based on folktales. The stories are mainly from Norwegian lore. Some aspects are based on the original stories while other parts have been expanded and added to. This four part series is meant to take the series and expand it to an epic tale.

Mullins

The Polar Bear King

Before

Jorgen gathered his climbing gear for early the next morning. He was determined to make his way to the mountain before the storm that was due later in the week. As he packed, his son Kristoffer watched intently, his eyes were filled with wonder and dreams of the climb. He wanted so badly to be at his father's side as he reached the top of the mountain.

"Papa, I want to go this year. I have practiced, I wouldn't be in your way." The boy pleaded.

"Kristoffer you are only nine. You would not be able to climb the rocks and hold the ropes as I do. I have told you many times when you are older I will take you." Jorgen looked deep into his son's eyes and saw the hurt, but he knew there was no way he could take him. "Now off to bed with you, it is past your time, your mother will blame me for keeping you so late.

Jorgen ushered the boy to bed and then looked in on his daughter who slept in the next room. Gerda was sound asleep; she had no desire to climb mountains. Her life was filled with books and learning. He walked over to her bed and leaned in to kiss her on the forehead. She just curled up tighter and clung to her blanket. The fire in the house provided a barrier to the frozen valley around them, but when the wind blew, you could feel the house's every crack.

"Jorgen if you keep watching your daughter sleep, you will never get any sleep yourself." Freya whispered smiling at her husband.

"I know, sometimes I can't help myself, she reminds me so much of you. She'll break hearts one day, just like you did."

"I never set out to break hearts; I just captured the one I wanted. Now, if only I could convince you to stay home tomorrow. I don't want you to go." She lowered her eyes so Jorgen could not see her pain.

"Freya, I have climbed so many mountains. I will be fine, you'll see."

Jorgen checked the house and made sure the fire would last as he headed to bed. Freya watched, unable to speak of the real feelings she had inside. She bore a secret that she dared not tell anyone not even her husband. She knew what was at the top of the mountain, but telling him might open up a bigger, more destructive secret. Silence was her only option for now and a hope he would not be able to reach the mountain peak or find the castle.

Freya did not sleep the entire night, she just lay there and watched Jorgen. She loved him more than anyone she had ever known. He was her family before the children came along. She had tried so hard to leave behind her birth family. Only her sisters remained, and she wanted nothing to do with them.

It had been nearly a decade since she left the mountain top and renounced her powers. She ran it all through her head over and over again. There had to be some fragment of her abilities left that could protect him on his journey. If she could only keep him from harm, she would use the power again. As she looked over at the bedside table, she saw the broach. Her mother had given it to her as a girl. She treasured it; it was the only part of her past she allowed to remain.

The Polar Bear King

As she held it in her hands, she ran her fingers over the rose flower shapes that made up its intricate design. "This will have to do." She whispered. Waving a hand over it, the familiar tingling ran through her fingers. A warm glow extended from her hand and engulfed the broach. The light was bright and red in color but it did not awake Jorgen. She smiled as she realized the power was still within her.

As she watched the power fill the broach, she whispered a spell of protection. And then she knew, she had accomplished her goal. Freya quietly slipped out of bed and went down to where her husband had left his equipment. As she looked it over, she saw the side pouch of his pack. It was there she hid his protector. She turned her head upwards, "Mother I promised I would never part with this, but I have to make sure he is safe. If you are watching, please make sure he comes back safely."

The morning came just as Freya finished her mission. She knew Jorgen would be up and leaving soon. As she went to the kitchen to prepare his food, her heart ached. This was wrong and she knew letting him leave, would not result in anything good. She also knew, she would not be able to stop him. When he made his mind up to do something, it could not be changed. This was the first time she wished she could.

Jorgen came down and ate as he watched Freya. He knew she was troubled but she would never tell him. He smiled at her as she walked past. As he extended a hand, she took it and looked him in the eyes. "I'll be alright." He tried to reassure her. It didn't work; she knew all too well how dangerous it was to go near the castle.

The Polar Bear King

Jorgen started to leave for his climb when the sun was just up enough to see. He kissed Freya and waved good-bye. As he started his climb, he never looked back. His mission was to reach the top of the mountain before evening. He took the rugged rocks quickly and showed how his years of climbing made him an expert.

Stopping along the way to rest, he would look back and survey the valley below. More than once he was sure he saw something behind him, but after several hours he put it out of his mind. Maybe it was the altitude playing tricks with his mind. He stopped looking back by the afternoon, as he got to the high peaks. If he had looked back again, he might have seen his son Kristoffer making his way just minutes behind his father. The boy had been right; he was able to handle the climb.

The evening came and Jorgen reached the top of the mountain. He looked around him to take satisfaction in his accomplishment. It was then he saw it in the distance; a large structure of sleek and shimmering ice. It was a castle hidden at the very peak of the mountain, not visible to the valley below. He studied it as he walked the slope that led to the entrance.

The outside looked like an architectural dream. The walls surrounding the grounds were flawless. The gate was carved ice, as if done by a true craftsman. As he touched the gate it swung open effortlessly. Jorgen was hesitant about entering, he did not want to trespass, but he wondered who could live in a castle of ice. No human could exist there. He entered and walked through the middle of the garden. The flowers there were all made of ice resembling perfect delicate sculptures. No two were alike; they all had been carefully constructed to be flawless.

As Jorgen approached the steps to the huge doors that protected the front of the castle, he called out hello but no one answered. He continued to move up to a point that he could knock. As his hand touched the door it swung open. His heart almost stopped from fear of who or what might occupy the castle. His courage was not enough to take him inside. He backed down the steps where he originally came and to the side. Not realizing what he was doing, he stepped on one of the perfect flowers and it shattered.

The sound of the flower shattering rang throughout the mountain like a bell. Jorgen realized what he had done. He had to go in now and apologize. He just didn't know to whom. As he looked around, he did not notice that someone else had already become aware he was there. Far above on a balcony of the frozen castle, Elaida watched. She had created the gardens and the castle. Her eyes looked on, enraged as she watched her unwelcome visitor.

Kristoffer made his way to the gates of the castle, looking on in childlike amazement. He did not know things like this ever existed. He had never been taught it in school or dreamed it possible. He worked his way through the garden, as his father once again approached the door. Jorgen knocked again and when no response came he stepped inside. Kristoffer was not far behind as he watched his father set down his pack by the door and walk to the large opening where a crystal looking staircase and chandelier engulfed the room.

Jorgen looked around at the decorations that adorned the hall. There were eleven statues made of ice that lined the walls. Each one was unique and carved with specific human features. All so lifelike and at the same time too perfect he thought. He had never seen such work in his life.

"Hello, is anyone here?" He called out and waited for an answer.

"And what do we have here?" A voice came from the top of the steps...

"I am sorry for the intrusion. I wanted to apologize for stepping on one of your flowers." Jorgen continued.

As the female walked down the steps Jorgen could see she was a beautiful woman with very white features and a long flowing sheer gown. Her eyes never left him, as she made her way down step by step. A sinister look covered her face. She looked at him as if she was a wild animal and he was her prey. She stopped several steps from the bottom landing. Elaida liked to be above the ones she spoke to; it gave her an air of power. That is also why the castle was located at the highest peak in the area.

"So, you destroyed one of my creations?" Elaida said lowering her head and glaring.

"I didn't mean to, I was backing down the steps and I stepped backwards onto one. I am so sorry I know these creations must be time consuming. They are so beautiful." He smiled at her.

"So you like my work?" She spoke while looking at him with a psychotic expression.

"Yes, I especially like these statues. They are like nothing I have ever seen. How did you get the expressions so perfect?"

"Fear does a lot when someone is modeling for you. They just need motivation."

The Polar Bear King

She said as she descended the steps and began to walk circles around him.

"Why fear? What is there to be afraid of?" He asked.

"Well…me of course. Do you not find me frightening?" Elaida laughed out loud.

"No, you are very beautiful."

"Flattery… that could almost get you forgiven for destroying my work. You are quite a beautiful man. I have captured so many different looks and body types in my work, but never a man built like you. So many muscles and that handsome face. You could almost melt a girl's frozen heart." She spoke as she continued to walk around him running a fingertip over his chest.

"Thank-you I appreciate the compliments." Jorgen said uneasily.

"Not so much compliments, mostly me thinking out loud. I could use a new statue. It has been years since anyone made their way up the mountain. You must be quite the climber; the way is so icy and slick. But then it is supposed to be to keep prying eyes out of my castle."

Kristoffer listened intently trying to understand what was going on. The woman frightened him. She did not seem normal. Her skin looked as if it was made of ice. He managed his fear and waited to see what his father did.

"Do you live here alone?" Jorgen asked.

"Yes, I have for decades, since my parents died and my sisters went to their own domains."

"Aren't you lonely?"

"No, I have my friends here to keep me company."

"I am Jorgen, what is your name."

"My family called me Elaida. I have been known by many other names over the years. Maybe you have heard of me by reputation. How does the name Snedronningen strike you?"

"You are the Snow Queen?"

"Yes, I see you have heard of my bad reputation. People seem to misunderstand me so much, they have labeled me as frozen. I am so much more than that I am ice and destruction. I am a goddess. And you…are less than that."

Jorgen turned to look at the door. He was ready to run, but it was too late. The Snow Queen raised her hand and the ice entered through his feet. He couldn't move. Kristoffer looked on in fear at the fate of his father.

"You will be my latest masterpiece. I only had eleven before, now you complete my dozen. So handsome, I might have liked you, if my heart was not filled with ice. Now…join my collection."

Jorgen's whole body froze solid as his son watched. In a panic, Kristoffer stood up to run just as the Snow Queen spotted him. She turned loose a flurry of snow in his direction. Like a swarm of killer bees, they flew in his path like they had a mind and a purpose. As he ran, Kristoffer tripped over his father's pack and on the ground fell the broach his mother had put in. He knew what it was and picked it up as he scrambled to the door.

Just outside, the swarm of snow swirled around him. Kristoffer held tight to the broach as the bees touched his skin and piece by piece melted from the warmed air that surrounded him. The Snow Queen watched the magic taking place. "He has been charmed." She screamed. She recognized the broach and a rage soared through her. Her sister was still alive.

Mullins

The Polar Bear King

Chapter 1: A New King on the Throne

The lands in the valley had always been prosperous and times were once good during the rule of the elder King Valeman. That was before the Witch became aware of the kingdom. As Prince Valeman was away in other parts, his father fell under her control. She warped his mind in a way he would only respond to her and obey her orders.

The kingdom fell into ruins under her control. The people suffered cruel and unusual punishment. The strain of the witch's power took a horrible toll on the Kings health. He did not live long after. The Queen sent out word by messenger to her son to return home and take his rightful place on the throne. Weeks passed but there was no sign of the Prince. The Queen managed to rule in his absence but the state of the kingdom only worsened. When the prince did return home, there was little to return to.

As the Prince made his way to the home of his mother, he saw the destruction around them. He was heartbroken, not only for his father but his people as well.

"Mother how did this happen? How did everything fall apart like this?" The Prince pleaded for information.

"Your father was beguiled by the Witch from the North. She came here and befriended him. In doing so, she gained his trust and then she cast a spell on him to only trust her. She destroyed everything with her demands and abuse of the people." Queen Valeman lowered her head to hide her tears from her son.

The Polar Bear King

"It's OK mother, I will make this right. The Witch will not find it so easy to control me."

The young Prince hugged his mother. He didn't know how, but he would save his people. But first, he had to lay his father to rest. He sent out word to all corners of the land that he was back and the funeral would be held immediately. People came from every village and town to say good-bye to the man they once loved. It all seemed so unreal that he could have been pushed over the edge both mentally and physically.

After the ceremony, the Prince called upon all who had come, to return to the town center to participate in his coronation. The time for a new King, was well past due, he told them. Some were skeptical that he could undo the damage caused to them. Others were willing to believe in anything that freed them from the Witch's power.

As the crown was placed on the head of the new King, the crowds cheered. There was a feeling of release and hope. In all the excitement, no one witnessed the Witch who was looking on from the trees nearby. Many did however notice the cold air that swirled down the hill. As she watched, the Witch stared intently at the new King. She studied his handsome face and chiseled jaw line. She admired his blond hair, cut ever so shortly and the muscles throughout his body. 'He would make a fine husband.' She thought.

She hid behind the guise of an old woman as she made her way near him. As she passed through the crowd, she seemed pleased with herself that it all came so easily. 'If they only knew the Snow Queen was this close to them, they would run and hide in their trashy hovels.' She thought to herself. She walked all the way up to the King with no resistance.

Pleased with herself for getting as far as she did, she knew she still had to get him alone. As she passed by the platform he stood on, she greeted him and just as he extended his hand to her, she fell to the ground. She seemed helpless and ill. Just as she had hoped, the ruse worked, for the King ordered two of his men to escort her to his private chamber to rest and have water. As the King arrived and his men left, the old woman stood up.

The King stepped back in shock, he did not understand. Then the old woman transformed into her true self. The rags she wore fell to the ground and she stepped forward in a beautiful gown and revealed herself as the Snow Queen. The King studied her for a moment and then realized she was the witch everyone spoke of.

"So you are the one who corrupted my father and destroyed the kingdom? Valeman leered at her.

"Destroyed…is such a harsh word. Maybe we should say I used the Kingdom for my own benefit." She laughed evilly as she stared him in the eyes.

"So, you think it is Ok to just show up one day and plunder what is not yours?"

"If it suits my purposes…why not?" She studied him intently looking for his weaknesses.

"Your time here is done. I am in charge now and it's your time to leave."

The Snow Queen laughed out loud, "You just don't know what I am capable of. Push me again…and you will find out the hard way."

The Polar Bear King

"What do you want? There isn't anything here anymore that you can take, the land is barren, there is no fortune to be found. The people have nothing."

"I wouldn't say there isn't anything I could want." She spoke in a sexy voice, as she walked around his back running her hand over his shoulders.

The king felt the chill run through his bones. He realized then, why she was called Snow Queen. His heart sank as he finally began to understand her desires. She wanted to be a Queen to his King. A merging of the two of them, to create a master kingdom. With him at her side, she knew they could conquer any enemy.

"There would be no kingdom that could defeat my frozen army of ice warriors and polar bears."

"You are crazy, we are a peaceful people. We do not war against those around us. We work to better ourselves and our friends." The King insisted.

"Your father understood my desires. It was easy to sway him; I could show you how I did it. You might even enjoy it." She whispered in his ear as he tried to resist her advances. "Now, be a good boy and I will make you very happy."

"Not a chance in hell, I will never marry you and you will never control this land again!"

"Never say never…sweetheart! I tried to do this the easy way, and you just had to be a bad boy. Now…suffer at the hands of a true Queen. By light one way, by night another. Your form will change, you will soon discover. By day a beast of a bear you will be, at night a man while others sleep. To break this spell you must achieve, the love of another while being the beast." She clapped her hands as she finished the spell sealing his fate. "Now go and find true love, if you can, and if for seven years after you find this love the person does not look upon your human form you will be a man only. If they do look upon you as a man, you are mine to take."

"What did you do to me? What does all of this mean?" He demanded answers.

"It means my darling handsome boy, when you come to your senses and agree to marry me the spell will be ended. If you do not, for the next seven years by day you will be a smelly…nasty…polar bear. At night…you will be a man. If you can find someone to love you as a bear, then in seven years you are your old self again. The spell will end. It's not hard to understand. Now, wouldn't it just be so easy for you to change your mind?"

The King looked at her in disbelief. "You can't just make me change into a polar bear. It's not possible."

"Want to bet on that one? I have so many powers you would not believe. I can create ice and snow, I can cast spells to get things I want, and I can even damage your life more than you could ever imagine possible." With her last words, the expression on her face changed completely to rage. She knew she was not going to win this fight.

She backed up a few steps as she stared hard at the King. He felt a strange sensation in his hands. His fingernails began to darken and white hair started to sprout out of his skin. His face stretched and distorted, as did much of his body, as he let out a blood curdling scream. As he fell to the floor, his body mass increased and his clothes ripped away. He rolled over face down as his body transformed completely into a bear.

As he rose up, the remnants of a human male were gone. He was now a beast. He turned to the Snow Queen, and in a rage prepared to rip her limb from limb.

"Now…now, temper will get you nowhere. And if you kill me, you will still be under my spell for seven years. Now don't you think you should be a good boy and change your mind?"

The King growled loudly, sounding like a tormented animal. He knew he could not give in. He would have to find another way to break the spell. He turned, as if to aggressively rush at the Snow Queen, but she blew the full force of a winter storm in his direction and he fell to the floor.

"Nice try my love, but you will have to be faster than that to get to me." She walked over to him and formed an ice block to hold his feet together. "I think it is time for me to leave. A girl has to take care of herself, and you seem a little too hostile right now. I'll give you some time to think about your future, then we will talk again. Just…stay cool until then. "She laughed as she left the palace and the Polar Bear King.

The Polar Bear King

Chapter 2: Rise of the Polar Bear King

King Valeman sat upon the floor of his chamber. He still could not believe what had happened to him. He shook his huge white head back and forth. His actions were still clumsy; he was not used to his new form. He tried to stand up and was wobbly at first. When he learned to stand on all fours it came easier to him.

"This was easier when I was pissed off." He growled in his deep throated voice.

He walked over to the dressing mirror and stared at his appearance. He had really transformed to a large white bear, there was no denying it. His mind raced, trying to conceive some way of returning to his former self. He did not know magic or anyone who could perform such acts of this level. His only chance for living a normal life was to find love and wait seven years.

Since no one knew of what happened, he stood behind his door and called out for a servant to bring his mother. He knew this would not be easy. If he stayed hidden while he talked to her, she may just believe it was him in the form of the bear. There was no other way. One thing he knew for sure, he would have to leave the palace and the kingdom, without anyone knowing he had changed.

His mother arrived and upon entering the room called out for him. From behind a dressing blind, he spoke to her.

"Mother, I need to tell you something, and you need to understand what I am telling you is truth. Do you understand?" He asked her.

The Polar Bear King

"Yes my son, I trust you. Tell me what is wrong?"

"The witch came back. She demanded I marry her. I refused and she put an enchantment upon me. I am no longer as I was." His voice trailed off in a scratchy gruff tone.

"What did she do to you? What has happened to your voice?" The Queen became terrified.

"She cursed me to be in the form of a Polar Bear, if I find true love after seven years I will return to being a man. If not I will be this way forever. Mother, I have to leave here and go far away to resolve this. It is too soon after father's passing for the people to endure this. If the kingdom is to survive, I must leave for a time. You can rule in my absence. Since the witch is no longer here you will be able to rebuild what was destroyed."

Valeman's heart sank as he told his mother of his plans. He knew the task he had burdened her with was great, but he had no choice. It would be dangerous to have him stay there. His mother bowed her head down as tears ran from her cheeks. It was too much too soon, she had just laid her husband to rest and then to have to lose her son so quickly was insane.

As she cried, Valeman could not stand the pain he heard. He walked out from behind his hiding place and the Queen looked up and screamed. She was terrified at the sight before her. Her son really had been changed but she was not prepared.

"Mother please, it is still me in here…just changed."

The Polar Bear King

"You are a beast, a great white bear. I am sorry; I was not prepared for the site of this."

"I know mother, and imagine what our people would say if they were to see it. I cannot rebuild the kingdom if the people fear me or just see me as the Polar Bear King. I do not want to rule a people in fear of me. I must go for a time, but I will return when I find a solution to this."

"Where will you go my son? Where will you be safe?" The Queen became scared for his safety.

"I don't know. I guess I will have to travel to the Winterland, the Kingdom of Ice and Snow. It would seem the appropriate place for a bear such as me."

He drew a deep breath and sighed. There really were not very many other options but to leave everything he knew behind. He told his mother he would leave that evening. It would be easiest then, since he would return to human form and be able to leave the palace without arousing suspicion. He felt a lump in his throat, for he knew after this, he would never be the same again.

As night spread across the land, he looked out upon the balcony. The rays of the moon shone in, and as one hit his paw, the transformation began. "By light one way, by night another." He whispered the words as he transformed into the man he had once been. As the moonlight coated his body, he stood there naked by the balcony. He looked at his skin and remembered what it was like to be a human.

He walked to the mirror and stood there. His mind raced over what had happened and he wondered for a moment should he have given in to the Snow Queen. All would be resolved if he did. As he stood there thinking, he did not notice the snowflakes which began to fall on the balcony or the approach of the woman who came with them.

"I think I like you just as much with your clothes off." The Snow Queen laughed.

"Don't get used to it. This is as close as you will ever get to me naked in a bed chamber." The King snarled as he tried to conceal his nakedness.

"Ha, don't be ashamed sweetheart, I am actually impressed. You have nothing to be embarrassed about."

"Why have you come back? Did you feel the need to ridicule me?"

"No, I thought you might want to reconsider your position."

"Go to hell witch." He screamed at her.

The Snow Queen lowered her head as she looked at him with rage in her eyes and screamed, "Don't call me a witch, I am so much more than that. I am Ice, I am Snow, I am a Goddess to be worshipped. And you are nothing more than a Polar Bear King. And that you shall stay until the enchantment has run its course."

The Snow Queen turned and walked towards the open balcony doors. As she stepped out, she turned and looked at him one last time. "Such a pity, we could have had so much fun together. Now, the time for fun is over. I think you need to learn how to suffer." With her last words, she rose off the balcony, boarded her ice craft and flew off into the night leaving a trail of frost on the ground below her.

The Polar Bear King

The King dressed and gathered a few things he could take in a pack with him for the journey. His mother returned to see her son off. She placed a chain around his neck that her husband had given to her as a memento of love and protection. Her son had only returned and now she had to say good-bye again. She knew it had to happen. There was no chance for him if he stayed. The King walked down the steps of the palace and climbed on the back of his horse. He rode as fast as he could to the edge of the land and it was there he dismounted. He patted the loyal horse on its back and told it to return home. "The rest of this journey…I go on alone."

Mullins

The Polar Bear King

Chapter 3: The Winterland

The Winterland was a kingdom of snow ice and always cold. It was far to the north and few ever went there on purpose. Those who were born there, were used to the cold feel of the terrain. The King of the Winterland, was well loved by his subjects and rightfully so, for he protected them and made sure all were well taken care of.

The King was not alone for he had three daughters. The two older daughters were a bit homely but the youngest was quite beautiful and had many suitors. Since the Queen's passing, the King was very protective of his daughters and would not just let any man court them.

As the Polar Bear King approached the land of ice and snow, he saw the caravan of sleds heading for the north. They blasted past him quickly and unknowing of his existence. It was probably better they did not see him for furs and pelts were very sought after in the cold environment. A large coat of polar bear fur would probably have fetched a high price. The Polar Bear king watched as they faded into the distance and he continued his journey forward.

As the group of sleds wound through the forest, they picked up speed. The woodlands had the reputation of being a haven for wolves. It was a reputation that was about to be proven. As the sleds reached the halfway point of their journey, the wolf pack was aware of their presence.

From behind the trees, the wolves ran out at top speed throwing snow and ice from their path. They didn't travel in small numbers. They numbered more than fifty.

The Polar Bear King

Before the men could take notice of them, more than twenty wolves were closing in on the sled in the rear. The cry of the silver haired alpha male told them of their impending doom.

The land was frozen and food was scarce. The wolves were hungry. Anything that moved was fair game to them and the men looked like a sizeable prize. Today the meal was man. The wolves howled as they closed in on the last sled. The driver looked back in fear as he could hear the growls that were closing in on his heels.

As the closest wolf leaped at the back of the sled the driver turned his whip and slammed it into the wolves head. The beast screeched out in pain as it flew back into the pack knocking several of the wolves to the ground and disrupting their pace. The others rebounded, determined to claim their prize.

As the sleds flew around the steep trail, they hit a downhill slope towards the valley that lay before them. Their speed increased, and they flew down the steep slope leaving the wolves behind. The last driver looked back in relief as he realized he had survived the threat of being eaten alive.

As the sleds came to a stop at the edge of the small village, the town's people who were gathered outside grouped around them. The leader of the group Malachi was not one to pass up an opportunity to make a sale. He had survived the wolves and for him that meant it was a good day. As the people looked on, he pulled out his items for sale and went into his routine.

The people of the town were isolated and welcomed strangers, especially ones who could sell them things that were not readily available in the middle of winter. Malachi made many sales that day but also made sure to keep back several choice items for the King of the Winterland.

~

The polar bear king walked on, down the lonely path he had chosen. He feared contact with men who would be too quick to kill him. But he would not be able to avoid them forever. As he walked deep in thought, he did not notice the snowflakes that circled around his head or feel the frigid drops that froze in his hair.

As the wind increased he was torn from his deep thought. He knew this freak storm that had come upon him was not normal. He looked around in all directions trying to find the source of the frozen blast. As he turned his head to look over his left shoulder he saw her. The Snow Queen had returned.

"So, you have returned to try to tempt me?" He growled in a deep throated breath.

"Who me? I would never." She laughed as she calmed the storm she had encircled him with. "I only wanted to find out if you had come to your senses yet."

"I could kill you with one swat of my paw. Does that tell you how I feel?"

"Temper, temper. Mustn't upset the one who can freeze you solid. Come to think of it, I don't have any animal statues in the great hall. But no, I have other plans for you."

"Your threats do not scare me. You see you have done something unthinkable to me already. But I still survive. I will break this curse or it will run its course. I win either way, but you will never get what you want." The Polar Bear King laughed as he finally saw a bright point in his unfortunate existence. He continued on with his journey.

~

Malachi and his men stayed the night in the village. They ate and found warm beds and for that they were grateful. Exhausted from the chase of the wolves, no one had any trouble sleeping.

The next morning they were up early and on their way to Winterland. They made their trip through the ice and snow-covered land quickly and reached the outer gates of the king's village by late afternoon. The sleds flew up the path and to the outer doors where the king had already been alerted to their arrival.

As Malachi stood up and walked towards him, the king was very happy to see him and his team. He walked over to them, and the king reached down and patted the lead dog on the head. As he surveyed them, he realized the animals were tired from being driven hard. He ordered one of his men to take the animals into the kennel area where they could have food and water.

"Malachi, I was worried about you. I thought the wolves might have finally gotten their dinner." The king said hugging his friend.

"Jacob, I have no desire to be anyone's dinner. It'll be more than a pack of wolves that takes me down. We did stay in a village overnight; the chase was a bit rough. I am not getting any younger you know."

"Neither of us are my friend." The King laughed. "So what have you brought me?"

"Many wonderful things. Shall I bring them in now?"

The Polar Bear King

"My daughters and I will meet you in the great hall. They are just as excited to see what you have brought.

The King went to get the girls and bring them in to choose what items they wanted. The two older girls were picky as always. They just wanted what was expensive and unusual. They were spoiled and the King knew it. He really did not like them much, but he tried to overlook the way they turned out. And then Emily entered the room. She was beautiful and kind. Truly she was the opposite of her sisters. She was her father's favorite and the other girls hated her for it.

The two older sisters grabbed what they wanted and left the room without even a thank-you to their father. Emily took her time and complimented the men on the items they brought and was not greedy. She chose one thing, a picture of flowers; she then thanked her father for allowing her to choose. He smiled at her and as he looked at her face, he saw his wife. They were so much alike. Both were so beautiful that it was easy for him to be taken with his daughter.

Emily left the hall and walked past her sisters who were rummaging through they things that had grabbed. She glanced over at them for just a second but they were too busy in their own selfish fight over who got the most out of the visit from the men. Emily did not care for their fight; she just reached for her cape and threw it over her shoulders as she headed out the main door.

As she headed down the path towards the entrance to the village she looked up. She was sure she saw movement in the tree line in front of her. There it was again. She knew she was sure. The figure looked like a large white bear. But bears never ventured into

The Polar Bear King

Winterland. Polar Bears were forbidden to come there and stayed in the Iceland to the north.

She called out to the bear to try to get his attention. As she did he looked up at her. She was so lovely, he thought to himself. He wished he were still human, if he was, he could go to her. But he was the Polar Bear King and what lovely girl such as she could ever love a beast such as him. Emily watched as he continued on his way. She smiled, for she thought he was a beautiful bear. She walked on wishing she had known where he was headed.

Mullins

The Polar Bear King

Chapter 4: Changes

As Emily looked out of the window of her bed chamber, she wished upon the moon. She longed to be somewhere else other than where she was. The Winterland was her home but she dreamed of a land with sun and flowers. She knew somewhere this land existed, and there would be a man she would love. As she sat on her bedside she held the picture that she had received from the merchants. She didn't realize that the land she dreamed of really did exist.

As she dreamed, she saw a garden and trees covered in flowers in the Summerland and a man walking through them. As he moved about she saw him clearly in her mind's eye. She called him Valeman. He was a handsome man in his early twenties, youthful and kind. Emily had no idea he was a real man or that her dream would eventually come true. She did not realize she had already met Valeman or that he had become the Polar Bear King.

~

As the Polar Bear king walked through the woods, he thought back to the happier days in Summerland. He missed his mother. He knew this time was hard on her. She was strong, stronger than most would have given her credit. His mind traveled back to the day of the funeral and the gift his mother had given him. The chain his father had given his mother. A sign of pure love, she said it was to be given to the one he intended to marry. He now wore it around his neck as a reminder that one day he would be human again and know love.

The Polar Bear King

As the darkness of night covered the land, he felt the change begin. His body lifted into the air and spun as he was engulfed in light. As he spun his body returned to its former state. He landed back on the ground and was a man again; a cold man, standing naked in a dark frozen forest. He quickly pulled clothing and boots from his pack.

As he dressed he thought to himself that as he was to change at night and in the morning, he would have to be quick to not destroy these things as the bear would rip through his only clothing. He laughed to himself; the whole concept was so crazy. How could he have ever come to this? Fully dressed, he walked on aware than as a man in the frozen cold of the night he could die. For a moment he forgot he was not the only animal in the woods. While he was still a bear he saw the wolves, now as a man he stood no chance against them.

As the snow fell down heavier than before, the temperature dropped to a point that his hands began to feel frozen. Valeman knew he had to find a shelter, some place of safety. He scanned the area and saw the rock formation through the trees. It was like a cutout in the wall of stone. It was not a perfect solution, but it would shield him from the snow, and a fire would stop him from freezing to death.

He made his way over as fast as he could without losing sight of his surroundings in what had become a blizzard. He could barely see as he came to the opening. He sat down his pack, and heard a noise he was not prepared for. In his haste to get to protection, he did not see the wolf pack closing in on him.

The Polar Bear King

Valeman turned to face them, and the alpha male came close as he sniffed in his direction. The animal cocked his head in a confused way. He saw man, but smelled polar bear. The wolf backed up two steps. He knew fear from tangling with the other polar bears that lived nearby. They were fierce warriors and did not back down in a battle. A fight with a polar bear meant death. Valeman recognized the fear in the wolf and knew it was his only advantage. He lunged like a bear and made the loudest roar he could. His ruse worked, the pack ran as fast as they could.

Valeman sat down and gathered the wood for his fire. As he thought about it, he realized the wolves did rely on scent and then he smelled himself. Even he knew, his smell was quite overpowering. He stacked the wood, lit a bit of kindling underneath and in time had a roaring fire. He was sure this night he would not die.

~

Emily awoke early the next morning. She and her sisters were eager to go out into the hills for skiing. The fresh snow always made for an exciting day. She bid her father good-bye and went down the slope to where her sisters awaited her.

As the sisters flew across the land, the older girls left Emily behind, as they always did. It was no secret they did not care for her. They knew she was their father's favorite and they could not compete. Jealousy ran deep in the girls since Emily had favor and was the most beautiful.

The two older sisters went on, and Emily found her own way. She was happy to be alone and think. She daydreamed often,

The Polar Bear King

and most of the time it was about escaping her life. As she made her way, she admired the trees, each one covered in an icy coat. The storm had made the whole region look as if it were carved from a huge block of ice.

~

Valeman had arisen early trying to save his clothing from the bear he would become. His enchantment was becoming a game to him. The changing was less traumatic now. He felt a bit of pain but it was less of a shock. He knew it was inevitable. He was able to get his things packed away since he knew bear claws were not good for such things. The only thing that was constant from bear to man and back again, was the chain his mother had given him. It was big enough for both their necks and reminded him that there was hope.

The Polar Bear King moved on through the woods. He was sure if he kept traveling to the north, he would find the polar bear kingdom. The wolves knew their scent, so they must be somewhere near. He feared going there, but by day he would fit in. By night he would have to hide. What choice did he have?

As he thought to himself, he heard a noise. It came up quickly from the side path. Someone was coming and he had to get out of sight. As he turned to run, he let out a growl before he knew what he was doing. It was then Emily heard him. She knew the bear was near. She wondered if it was the white bear from the day before.

As she skied towards the sound, the Polar Bear King once again let out growls. They were loud and sounded angry. For a moment Emily thought she was in danger.

The Polar Bear King

Then the Polar Bear King Spoke and Emily heard the words of a man. She pulled her hands down from her ears and looked at the bear coming in front of her. Perhaps he was no bear at all.

"Don't be afraid." The Polar Bear King pleaded with her.

"Why are you so upset, are you hurt?" Emily asked "Are you really a bear?"

"I am not a real a polar bear, I am the king from the south." He responded. "I was put under a spell."

The Polar Bear King pulled at the chain around his neck and it flipped to the ground. As he pawed at it, he was able to lift it into the air so Emily could see it. She looked at the chain for she thought it was the most beautiful thing she had seen.

"What is that?" She asked. "It's beautiful."

"It was a gift from my mother. My father gave it to her and she gave it to me, I can only give it to the one I am going to marry." The Polar Bear King struggled to answer.

As Emily looked into his eyes she saw the love of the man captured inside the form of a bear. The eyes were familiar to her. She remembered them from her vision of the land of flowers. He was the king she dreamed of. She didn't understand how it was possible. The man was real and a king, but he was also a polar bear.

"It is you." Emily whispered as she raised the chain over her head and let it fall around her neck.

The Polar Bear King

"Go home for now, I will come for you another day. I have a journey to go on." The Polar Bear King said as he disappeared into the white background.

As the two older sisters returned from skiing, the King met them in the outside. He asked where their sister was. But all he got was a sarcastic "We don't know". The King became frantic, and he called to his men to search the woods for the princess was alone in the forest.

They searched the area nearest the homes, it was then Emily came out of the woods and approached the men. The King ran to her and asked her where had she been, but she pushed past him and entered the great hall. As she warmed herself by the fire, her father demanded to know what had happened. She told him of the beautiful white bear who was not really a bear at all, but a king under a great spell.

The King assured her that he was a wild bear and only wanted her for his next meal, but she insisted he was kind. She also told him that the bear wished to marry her. The King found it all to be utter nonsense. He told her there was no spell and her people did not believe in such things.

Emily removed the chain from her neck and showed it to her father. She told him the bear had given it to her. He was furious and would have no part of it. As he stormed out of the room Emily called to him.

"Father he said he would be back for me in three days."

"If he does come back we will chase him all the way back to the North Pole where he belongs."

The Polar Bear King

Chapter 5: Kingdom of the Polar Bear

As the Polar Bear King made his way north, he found his way to the North Pole. He watched as he began to see more and more tracks of other bears. The closer he got, the more tracks were scattered about the ground. And then he saw the icy gateway that lead to the opening of the polar bear kingdom.

He knew he was safe for a time, being it was early in the day and he would not change anytime soon. Deep inside, he was still very scared to be there. He wondered why he even came. These bears would not accept him and even if they did, who was to say they would be aware of the magic of the Snow Queen. They would probably not be able to undo what had happened to him.

The polar bear guards spotted him before he got anywhere near the entrance to the snow cave. He was surrounded by several bears much bigger than himself. Each one was wearing a coat of armor to shield them in battle. They looked to be a community of war. Valeman became more fearful, he wished he could just turn and run, his people were a peaceful group, he did not know how to fit in there. The guards escorted him to the ice throne in the back center of the great hall of ice. There, the ruler walked down and ascended his throne.

"Who or what have you brought before me." The ruler asked.

"He walked into the guarded area and followed without a fight." The head guard responded.

The Polar Bear King

The ruler stepped down and walked over to Valeman and sniffed him. "You smell like a polar bear and then again you do not. Who are you? Why are you here in my kingdom?"

"I am the Polar Bear King." Valeman answered.

The ruler flew into a rage and grabbed Valeman by the neck with a great white paw and threw him to the ground. As he climbed on top, the ruler sunk his claws into Valeman's chest. The ruler did not know whether to kill him on the spot or torture him. He stared for some time and then went into a rage again.

"I am the Polar Bear King. There is no other. I will ask again, who are you? And I would advise you to answer quickly before I stop caring who you are." The King growled.

"I am Valeman. I am the King of Summerland. A witch put a spell on me to turn me into this form. She called me the Polar Bear King. I must break the spell to become a man again."

The room went into uproar. The bears rose on their hind legs and roared so loudly, the sounded bellowed out of the hall. The true Polar Bear King pulled his claws from Valeman's chest. He looked at Valeman intensely before walking back to his throne.

"Silence!" He screamed to the other bears. "What was this witch's name?"

Valeman looked up and in a deep growling voice he spoke. "The Snow Queen."

The room went crazy again with the bears reacting in fear of the name they had just heard. Valeman didn't have to ask, he knew she had been there before. He rolled over and tried to stand up. He was hurt and his chest bled from the scratches the King had given him. He knew he had to stand and not show weakness. If he looked frail they would kill him.

"What did she do to you? Were you human?" Valeman asked.

"No not human, just average bears. We were free and went about our way in nature. Then she came." The King explained. "She experimented with us through magic until we became what pleased her. An army…for her warfare. She turned us into creatures of war and killing. We were peaceful before she came. Now, we kill on command."

"I'm sorry to know that. I came here looking for a solution to what she did to me. I guess you are just as cursed as I am. There is only one way to break my enchantment."

The King looked up at him. "And how is that? Do you know of a way to break the Snow Queen's hold on us?"

"On you no, I have no way of changing what she has done. On me however, the curse can be broken by true love for the beast I have become. I wish I could help you, help all of you. The only way I can see you will be free is if the Snow Queen is no more."

"Agreed, but until that time, we are creatures of war, just as you are a creature of peace. Guards, chain him to the wall until I know what to do with him."

The guards drug Valeman to the side of the hall and chained his legs. He hung there defenseless as the Shaman came to him and attended to his wounds. Valeman couldn't understand why the King had imprisoned him. He was in no way a threat.

"Just hold still and let the healing happen." The Shaman insisted as he chanted over the wound.

"Thank-you." Valeman whispered.

"For what?"

"For making me whole again before nightfall. I can't imagine being human and having my chest ripped open like that."

"I understand your point. You will be completely healed in a matter of moments. Which is lucky for you, since I can see you are already starting to change."

As the light began to engulf Valeman, the Polar Bear King and his group of bears gathered around. His body lifted up and jerked at the chains, but he could not break free. As he began to shrink in size the shackles fell to the ground. Valeman turned around in the air and took his true form. As the King watched he knew what Valeman said was true to his words.

"Clear the hall." The King called out.

"Could I have my pack please? I have clothing in it." Valeman asked.

From behind, a new voice entered the room. A familiar one that sent chills down both of their spines. "Don't be so quick to dress. I'm not embarrassed one bit. They say clothes make the man, well yours only hide your better features." The snow queen laughed as she walked into the hall.

With every step, the room chilled more. The walls of the hall frosted over as she moved forward. As she reached Valeman, he fumbled for his clothing and dressed as fast as he could. The feeling of frostbite had already started on his feet and hands. The King of the Polar Bears walked forward to shield Valeman as he finished dressing.

"Why are you here?" The King of the Polar Bears asked.

The Polar Bear King

"I have work for you. The fact that I find you have a new family member here is just a bonus. So, tell me Valeman, how's life in the wild? Being a bear getting you down yet?" She glared at him intensely.

"I'm just fine. I have actually gotten used to the change." He jabbed back at her.

"It could be over so easily. Just take my hand and make a vow." She cocked her head and smiled.

"I don't think so. I'm not much for colder climates."

"Whatever you wish. I can wait; I have all the time in the world."

When she turned away to the King of the Polar Bears she told him of her plans to invade a neighboring land. She had let the Northern Land stay free long enough. Now it was her time to claim a new kingdom. It was a place of ice and snow, she had to have it.

As she turned to leave, she looked at Valeman and blew him a kiss. She told him that she would see him around and then she left with an arctic blast of snow and cold. Valeman turned to the king. She was planning to take over the land near where Emily lived. His heart sank with fear; he had to get Emily out of there.

"Give me time to go there and get out someone I know before the war breaks out. I ask you for only this one thing."

"Valeman you have won my respect and that is not easy. We are kin in a way since we are both enchanted. So, I will give you this much. We have days before the attack. I have time to let you go. But before you do, I think there might be something else I can do for you."

The King of the Polar Bears walked back to the storage area behind his throne. He pulled out several pieces of armor. Then he walked back to Valeman and instructed him on how to put on each piece. By the time the king was finished, Valeman realized in bear form he would look like any other warrior in the group.

"King, I thank-you for your gifts and allowing me to save Emily, but why do you want me to dress me like this?"

"Because the armor you will be wearing also has an enchantment. The Snow Queen herself made these to give each polar bear a level of invincibility. When you are a bear and wearing yours, no one can hurt you. And I am guessing this, but maybe it can slow down the Snow Queen as well. So wear it at all times of the day. And one day if the opportunity is right, free yourself and all the rest of us from her evil." The King of the Polar Bears growled.

"I understand." Valeman finally had an advantage. He was grateful to the Polar Bear King. At first light of day, when he was a bear again, he would go for Emily and take her to safety. With his new armor maybe he could take her to Summerland with him. He could protect her and his mother. He turned to the king and the two walked out of the great hall together.

The Polar Bear King

Chapter 6: The Road Home

The morning came, and Valeman once again returned to his form of Polar Bear King. This time was different though, he felt more confident. He had armor and defenses and possibly a way out of his curse. If Emily could truly love him, then she would be able to free him.

He headed towards Winterland, not knowing what reception he would receive. As he approached the outer gates, he saw the reception would not be pleasant. The king's guards were waiting for him. All were ready and all had weapons. Valeman was glad he had armor but was a peaceful man and did not want to have to use it.

As the Guards watched outside, Emily awaited inside. The King came to her and at first did not speak. He sat down by the fire a saddened hurt man. He had lost his wife many years before, and though she was not dead, Emily would soon leave him too.

"Father, you do not understand what I am doing." Emily whispered.

"My girl I have known and loved you for seventeen years. How could I understand you better?" The King replied.

"Father, if you love me, then let me make my own choices. Trust me to do the right thing."

"No…never. I will kill that bear before I allow him to harm you."

"Father please, try to be reasonable. I know what I am doing and I do it of my own free will."

The Polar Bear King

"I will not give up my most precious possession." The King insisted.

"You will still have my sisters. They will be here for you."

The king paced back and forth. "No they are selfish creatures, who only care for themselves. You have seen that as well as I have. They do not care for me, or you for that matter."

Outside the gates, the wolves howled a warning that the bear had returned. The king heard them and knew it was time. Emily tried to leave but her sisters held her tight and would not allow her to leave. She watched from the window as The Polar Bear King approached.

The King joined his guards, as the order to attack was issued. They came at him in groups and used every weapon they could find. Nothing seemed to pierce his protective armor.

Remembering he was Valeman, he tried not to harm the men but they gave him no choice and he threw them hard to the ground. They meant him harm and they proved it by stabbing at him with spears and pitchforks.

In the end, the men retreated, they knew they were no match for the bear. The King returned to his daughters. Emily pleaded with her father to let her go to the bear, but he refused. Then the oldest sister went outside insisting she could talk to all animals and he would obey her. Pretending to be Emily, she climbed onto the bear's back and allowed him to take her away from the village.

When they made it a short way, the Polar Bear King realized he had the wrong sister and threw her off. He returned to the doors of the great hall where the guards had regrouped. As he approached they attacked. And for the first time, Valeman drew the blood of another. His

The Polar Bear King

great polar bear claws ripped at a man, then threw him as the other men watched in horror and ran back to the houses.

Emily watched from the windows but she was not afraid, she knew he was a peaceful loving creature. This blood was on the King's hands, not the Polar Bear King. As he reached the outer door the King came forth, sword in hand to finish the situation once and for all. As he stood at the door, the Polar Bear King rose up on his hind legs about to attack, when Emily ordered them both to stop.

Emily stepped forward and showed him she was ready to go. He let her climb upon his back and they turned south to head to Summerland. The king watched as they grew smaller in the distance. His older daughter came to his side and assured him everything was fine, that he did not understand. He pushed her aside. "It is you who do not understand. How could you? You care for nothing but yourself." A tear ran down his cheek as the King turned to go back to his throne.

As the Polar Bear King and Emily walked further away, the frozen wintery land faded around them and green trees began to take shape. A warmth Emily had never known, was surrounding her. She like the feeling of the sun on her face. The Polar Bear King turned his head to look at her as she ran her finger through his fur.

As they reached the outer limits of the kingdom, he was surprised that his people greeted him not as the Polar Bear King but as King Valeman. They all knew his story and of the curse. The queen had told them all when she feared he would not return. As the people watched him, they were pleased he had found the love to set him free.

The Polar Bear King

Chapter 7: Return of the King

Word passed quickly through the land of King Valeman's return. Of course, not everyone was pleased. Standing in the background watching was a hooded figure. Her anger grew with every step they took towards the palace. Valeman was happy to see home and be back to familiar surroundings but he feared for Emily. He knew the Snow Queen would not allow peace and he feared what she might do to his family. Life would be hard. He wondered how they would survive for seven years.

As Valeman walked through the gardens, Emily awoke to see she was surrounded by the flowers she had seen in her picture and dream. She found the place to be beautiful. In her heart she knew she was home. Her mind went back to her father. She missed him terribly. If there was a way, she would send him a message to let him know she was safe.

In the palace, the Queen greeted them and took Emily to her heart. She was still fearful of Valeman's curse, but she knew this might end it. The curse ruled their lives for the years to come. By day the Polar Bear King ruled and went about his kingdom. By night he was a man who could be seen by all but his bride. He came to her in the night after he took human form. No lights were allowed and she never looked upon his face. For if she even caught a glimpse of him, the Snow Queen could claim her prize.

In time the queen disappeared from the castle. She herself knew the ways of magic, though not as powerful as the Snow Queen. She cast a spell to be invisible, so she could watch over Emily and her children. She knew

The Polar Bear King

the Witch would come for them as they were born. She would not allow her grandchildren to come to harm.

Emily became pregnant soon after she arrived at the palace. Over the time of her pregnancy the witch never showed. The day came when she was to give birth; the bells rang out through the land to announce the baby's birth. Valeman returned home in polar bear form to find he had a daughter. Word was sent back to the King of Winterland, that he was a grandfather. He was overjoyed and longed to see his daughter once more.

The Queen came to the bed chamber where Emily rested and looked upon the baby. She smiled as she looked down at her but she also felt the anger building around the child. The Snow Queen would soon arrive. The Queen knew she had to protect the child. She removed it from the cradle and wrapped it in a cloak of invisibility so no one could find it.

As the Queen left the room, the balcony doors flew open. A blizzard of snow and arctic wind filled the room. As she walked into the room, The Snow Queen stared at Emily. She sized her up and admired her beauty. For a moment the witch felt envy, and then it turned to rage. This girl had sex with the man she wanted.

"Hello my dear. So you are the one he chose." The Snow Queen scowled. "You bore the child I should have had. I should thank you for taking the ordeal off my hands. But, I think I hate you too much for that. I have no power over you, but the child which was born from my curse shall be mine."

"No, leave her alone." Emily screamed as the Snow Queen approached the cradle.

The Polar Bear King

As the Snow Queen reached for the blanket she saw there was no child. She screamed out. "You may have won for now, but every time you give birth I will return. I will make you pay."

As Emily ran to the crib she saw the child was no longer there. She screamed for help, but no one could find the child. The Queen standing invisible to all watched over her, hoping she could understand it was necessary.

As the years passed there were more children born to Valeman and Emily. And with every one the Queen came shortly after birth and removed them. True to her word, the Snow Queen returned each time and grew more and more angry. She was losing her battle to obtain Valeman as her husband. With each child Emily grieved the other's disappearance; she began to feel she herself had been cursed.

Emily endured her pain, child after child, and over time became inconsolable. She grieved so much she turned from Valeman. He tried to visit her but she only thought of her loss. So much time had passed and she still did not know the face of the man she married. She felt empty inside and longed for home and her father. She wanted to go home. Valeman understood her need, but if she left, he felt she would never return. He felt doomed to be the Polar Bear King forever.

One day two men came to the door of the palace. They asked for Emily by name. When she came to her door, she saw Malachi and another tradesman she knew by face. They offered a gift sent from her father. She unwrapped the present he had taken such care to bundle himself. She opened fur after fur, each wrapped in a tied package shape. Within seven layers of fur, she found the last wrapping. As she opened it, there was a special shaped metal box.

Emily looked at it not knowing what it could be. As she opened it, she saw inside a glowing sphere of magical snow. She held it in her hands and lifted it to her heart. As she pulled it closer, she could feel the warmth radiating towards her. It was the love of her family and it filled the hole in her heart that her missing children had left.

Emily looked up and smiled at the men and thanked them for delivering her gift. They told her that the king wished she would visit. As she held the Sphere to her cheek, Valeman entered the door in the shadows. He told her to go to her father, but to not stay away too long. He hoped her love would bring her back to him and they would survive the curse together. He asked only one thing of her, that if her sisters offered her a present, that she not accept it.

The King drew back into his shadowy hallway. His heart sank, for he felt there was something that would destroy them both, waiting for her in the Winterland. He did not know what, but he was sure it would start with one of the sisters.

The Polar Bear King

Chapter 8: A Gift from the Winterland, / The Fall of the King

Emily set off on her journey back to Winterland, escorted by royal guards. Her mood lifted as she rode and anticipated seeing her father again. As her mind wondered, the journey flew past and before she knew it she was entering the outer gates and could hear the welcoming sounds of music played by the people.

As she dismounted the horse, the townspeople came to meet her. They gazed upon her and realized she was no longer the child that left them, now she was a grown woman. Emily's father and sisters greeted her with love and joy that she was with them again.

The night was upon them before anyone cared to admit it, and the King drifted into sleep in the great hall. Emily and her sisters gathered together in the eldest's bed chamber and talked about the Polar Bear King.

"So what's he like?" The eldest asked.

"He is kind and loving but he never lets me see his face. He comes to me at night or I see him in the day as the polar bear." Emily responded.

"Does he have something to hide?" The youngest sister asked.

"Maybe there is something wrong with his face. Maybe it is because he is so ugly." The Eldest laughed and teased her sister.

The Eldest sister went to the cabinet on the other side of the room and pulled out a box of her most prized possessions. As she sat it down on the bed, she said she had an idea. She pulled out of the box something she said would put an end to the mystery.

"What is it that you have that could help me?" Emily asked.

The eldest responded. "I got this the last time we had traders visit the kingdom. Watch as you strike it, a flame comes out. Use this to light a candle and it will put an end to your mystery. No one will ever know."

Emily was unsure as she took the gift and walked away. It seemed dishonest and she remembered the warning of her husband. But her curiosity overrode her promise. She wanted to know. As so, even though she made a promise to her husband, she still brought back a gift from her sister.

When she was home the desire to see Valeman's face was so overwhelming, she used the device to light a candle at her earliest opportunity. She looked upon his face and admired his handsome features. She was quite pleased, so much so that she leaned in closer, and as she did a bit of candle wax dripped over the side of the holder and landed on his forehead.

"What have you done?" Valeman flew into a rage. "Do you not understand that in just three months the spell would have been broken? Now I have to marry the witch."

Valeman leaped out of the bed and headed for the door. Emily tried to stop him but he pushed her to the side. His anger controlled him and his fear of being married to the Snow Queen. The king's mother and the children still invisible to everyone watched. There was no reason for them to stay invisible now she said and she led the children away.

The Polar Bear King

Emily was grief stricken; she knew she had to find a way to save Valeman. She ran from the palace and into the woods. As she wondered her mind went in all different directions and she became confused. She searched for some sign of Valeman's passage.

She wandered through the water and land until she came to a state of exhaustion. As she stood looking all around her, she heard the voices calling to her. They beckoned her to follow them. As she walked the voices echoed around her, encouraging her down a single path through the woodlands. She climbed through the trees and she was transported to a valley where she could see a castle on the top of a mountain.

Emily walked through the path before her and came upon a fire where an old woman and three children were gathered. She came closer as the old woman invited her to warm herself.

Emily did not recognize the woman as the Queen of Summerland since she had put a spell upon herself. The children were much older and she would not have recognized them as her own.

Emily asked if the old woman had seen King Valeman, and she said yes, he had been by there earlier that day. Emily in her crazed state, insisted on leaving to go after him, but the children stopped her. They told her she needed new clothes and the oldest child went to a bag and brought forth a pair of magic scissors. As she held them in the air and began to open and close them clothing began to appear as if it were being created new.

They gave her the clothes and insisted if she was to catch up with the king she would have to eat with them. A magic cloth was spread upon the ground and food appeared on it from out of the air. Emily smiled at the

The Polar Bear King

children for she had never seen anything like this before. She thanked them and ate.

As she was finishing her food, one of the children walked up with a special pair of boots. "You will need these if you are to make it up the summit." The Queen told her. "When you get to the top there will be someone there to help you.

With the magic scissors, cloth and the boots Emily made her way up the side of the mountain. The climb was easy for the magic in the boots allowed her to walk up the side of the cliffs. With every step Emily remembered the warning of the old woman that the boots must stay dry at all times or she would fall to her death and the witch would win. As she climbed, she made it to the highest peaks before the snow was all about her on the ground.

As she stepped onto the rocks of the peak, the snow had melted a bit from the warmth below and her boots touched the water. As she lifted her feet into the air, the boots fell over the edge, and bounced off cliff edges all the way to the bottom. Emily looked over the edge in fear of the great distance she had climbed. She felt the turning of her stomach and she flipped over onto her back as she tried to let go of the feeling of vertigo.

Composing herself, she sat up and looked towards the ice castle. It was near and she only had a short climb before she was there. The boots might have been gone but she was sure she could make the last of the journey. As she clawed at the rock face in front of her she reached up to steady herself. Just as she did, she saw a rope descend in front of her. She was scared, what if it was a trick. She didn't know what to do and then she heard the voice.

"Grab the rope, you fool girl, so I can pull you up. You can't hang here all day or the Snow Queen will see you." It was a man's voice, but not one she knew. "Hurry, the old woman sent me to help you. Now come on."

Emily grabbed the rope. The old woman had helped her so far, maybe she was still looking out for her. She held tight as the man pulled her to the top of the flat land. He reached out a hand and helped her stand up. "I'm Timothy, we don't have long to talk, we have to get you into the castle before you are seen."

"But what about you?" Emily asked. 'Why are you safe here?"

"I am working the ceremony tonight. The Snow Queen brought in a few of the locals to celebrate her marriage. At the end of the ceremony she intends to wed King Valemen."

"No, we can't let this happen." Emily became angry.

"Then come on and let's get you out of site. Once inside we will dress you like a servant and she will probably not recognize you."

"But she has seen my face." Emily blurted out.

"She never looks at servants, we are beneath her. She thinks of herself as a goddess. The bitch would kill us just as soon as look at us." He turned away as the anger in his voice grew. "Now move it girl."

Chapter 9: The Wedding Ceremony / The Power of the Mirror

"You are just in time. The wedding is hours away." Timothy said in a grim voice.

"I have to talk to him and try to get through." Emily interrupted.

"Here, put these on and we will go to the tower where she has him locked in." Timothy handed her boots to protect her feet from the ice and snow.

"But what about the Snow Queen, will she see us?"

"Not if we go quickly, she is busy with greeting her guests for the ceremony. They have already started to arrive. All sorts of evil looking characters, one looked like the devil himself."

~

The Snow Queen walked down the grand ice covered staircase. She played the part of royalty well. The guests lined up at the bottom to be received by her. She worked her way down the line to the last and most important guest.

"Damian, you have never looked better."

"Thank you. But it is a bit cold here for my taste. I prefer a hotter environment if you know what I mean."

"To each his own hell my dear. I prefer the cold; it's just in my nature to be frozen." She laughed as she took his hand and they walked over to the large covered object just beside the steps.

"Is this it?" She asked.

The Polar Bear King

"Yes, this is my greatest creation. The mirror of power." He boasted.

"I must see it."

"Only if you can handle the effects of its honesty. Anyone who looks into it and gazes upon themselves will see their worst. The Mirror only reflects negative energy, but if it is used in the proper way, it is a great source of power, to control and rule." Damian smiled and looked her in the eyes.

"I must have it. Name your price." Her expression turned like an animal out for the kill.

"It is not for sale my dear. My demons will be taking it around the world on a tour soon. It's time the world got a little bit darker." He laughed

The Snow Queen turned from him and clinched her fist until her nails dug into the palms of her hands. A bit of blood seeped out but she never felt a bit of pain. She just glazed her palms over in ice and continued to run every idea through her head of how she could obtain the mirror.

~

Timothy covered Emily's head with a hat and instructed her on how to stand and walk like a boy. With the clothing she wore and her head covered, she looked good enough to fool the Snow Queen. As they approached the tower, Timothy had to depart, to go about his duties and sent Emily ahead with instructions of where to go.

She walked through the outer door of the tower, as she heard the Snow Queen. She was speaking out loud, as if she were casting a spell. Emily peered through the door, unseen as the she added ingredients and read from her Book of Shadows. She reached the last thing on the list, a touch of venom from a poisonous snake. She laughed as she added it to the brew. "This should make Valeman as nasty as me." She laughed even harder. "Then again no. No, no one can outdo me."

"I wouldn't say no one." Damian teased her. "Remember my girl, I have been in charge of evil since the beginning of time."

"Of course. Can't blame a girl for trying though."

Damian walked over to the podium where the Book of Shadows sat and flipped the pages back and forth. "What…my dear, are we cooking up here?"

"Oh, nothing special, just a little bit of evil to put someone in the right mood."

Damian smiled at her. "Be careful my dear, a little bit will control him, too much and he might become even more evil than you. He may be pretty, but if he kills you in your sleep, it really won't matter will it?" He threw his hands into the air and disappeared in a puff of smoke.

The Snow Queen fumed at his jab. She would have tried to kill him, but she was not strong enough to take on the devil himself. But if she had the mirror, that might make her strong enough to take on anyone. There would be no one who could resist her.

Emily drew back in fear; she had to find a way of stopping all this. The wedding could never happen. She thought about it for a few minutes. The Snow Queen was so vain, she would want to look perfect for her wedding, and Valeman as handsome as he was, might upstage her. The scissors could make clothing so beautiful the Queen would not be able to resist.

Emily sat down and made enough noise in the hall to draw out the Snow Queen. She used the scissors to make a shirt of the finest silk. The Queen came upon her and demanded the scissors, but Emily said they would only work in her hands. The Queen still thinking Emily was a boy, instructed her to make clothing for their wedding. She told Emily that she would have to make the dress for her and clothing for King Valeman. Emily insisted she would have to measure him first. The Queen agreed and Emily found her way in to him.

As Emily walked in front of the Queen, her shirt fell down a bit in the back. Her long blond hair started to come over the edge and the Queen saw. "For a boy, you have very long hair. Perhaps you are not a boy at all. You know you are much too late my dear, to stop anything." The Queen laughed.

    The Queen went ahead to Valeman and upon entering, pulled a bottle from her pocket. She made him drink from it, the potion she had made earlier. As he drank he became tired and fell over asleep. A servant brought in Emily to do the job she had been brought in to do. The Queen departed smirking at the fact she had just turned Valeman to the side of evil. Timothy entered and found them. He had seen the Snow Queen use the potion and told Emily. They were too late to save him.

The Polar Bear King

Chapter 10: Evil Can Work Both Ways

Emily refused to accept defeat, she returned to the room where she heard the Queen casting her spell. She watched as the Queen once again mixed a potion. This time, she mixed what would be a drink for her ceremony. Emily watched intently as the Queen read from the book. She knew this book was her only hope.

As the Snow Queen finished, she sat aside her potion and rushed off to prepare for the dinner that night. Emily walked in, saw the mixture and then read the book. The spell was there that was to turn Valeman evil. She read it intently, trying to make sense of it all. A little of the potion made a normal person evil. Too much of the potion, would strip the power of an evil person.

She turned and saw the pot that the drink had been made in, and then looked to the side at the potion of evil. If the entire contents of the potion were mixed into the drink, it would take out the entire reception party. But, it might just return Valeman to his normal self again. She quickly mixed the two together and ran away to return to the chamber where her husband was being kept prisoner.

~

The Snow Queen was waiting, as Emily returned carrying an arm full of clothing for Valeman to try. He was different now. He looked down at her as if she was a servant beneath his feet. The potion had worked well.

"Just leave the clothing on the bed. I will try it later myself, I don't want your dirty hands all over it." Valeman snapped at her.

"Now you sound like a man who is ready to rule the world at my side."

Emily pretended to be hurt and hid her face as she walked away. She headed to the kitchen to meet Timothy. He and the other staff prepared food for themselves. He complained of the poor rations they had. As Emily heard, she pulled out the cloth the old woman had given her. When she spread it upon the table and clapped her hands a banquet appeared in front of them and the servants were overjoyed.

The Snow Queen had been watching from a distance and came into the room. She saw the foods and that Emily had created them. She instructed Emily that she would make a meal for her guest that night, in celebration of the marriage. Emily agreed. She knew with the food, the Snow Queen would serve the drink she had made. The whole plan was coming together.

As the Snow Queen walked away Timothy ran to Emily's side. "You did it, you fooled her."

"Let's hope so. She still has to drink the potion to strip her powers. They all have to have it at the same time to make this work."

"They will have a toast at the beginning, to congratulate the couple, that should do it."

The meal time approached and every vile retched creature the Snow Queen had ever known, was entering the hall for the meal. As the horns blew a welcome, she and her future husband entered the room in the finest clothing anyone had ever seen. The Snow Queen was pleased, she wanted to upstage everyone there, and she did with her elegant dress.

The Polar Bear King

As the Queen sat down and quieted the room, she called for the servants to pour the wine. As they went around the room, the large vat of the mixture was more than enough to reach to every chalice. Emily, once again placed the cloth down the table, and clapped her hands and all sorts of exotic foods appeared before them.

The Snow Queen was pleased, as each guest drank their wine and ate of the food. No one knew what was really happening. Damian joined the party, late as usual. As he stood at the end of the table, he offered a toast for the merging of good and evil in the marriage of the Queen and Valeman. As they all drank, the potion did its job on everyone, except Damian and the Snow Queen.

Turning towards Emily, Damian stared at her. "Did you think a simple potion could take out the Prince of Darkness? If you did, you have another thing coming. He turned to the Snow Queen and glared at her. "I hold you responsible for this."

The Queen stood up and turned to Valeman. "Kill her. Kill her now!" She screamed.

"I'm sorry but I cannot do that. She is my wife and I love her."

"You were turned."

"Yes, I was, but the wine which turned everyone else, turned me back to what I always was."

The Snow Queen fumed as she walked away from Valeman. As she approached Emily she was totally enraged. She did not know who to strike down first. Her fascination with Valeman was gone. He betrayed her and Emily was nothing to her. She would be the first target.

"You think you won. But stupid girl, you did nothing to me. My powers are as intact as they always were. I am, and always will be a goddess. I am ice and power incarnate. I am now and will forever be the Snow Queen." She shouted and the walls quaked for a minute, before the whole castle felt her rage.

"You my dear are nothing." She turned towards Emily and let loose the full blast of her arctic wind and ice. As the shards ripped through Emily's skin, she was torn apart. Her body disappeared from sight in a matter of seconds. The Snow Queen looked on at the destructive power she had unleashed. "I correct myself, you are less than nothing."

"Very good my dear. I am impressed." Damian said looking on, as the frosty ice that blew through the room settled to the ground.

"Impressed enough to give me the mirror?" She said catching her breath.

"Not on your life…or over my dead body."

"I could arrange that." She laughed.

"Now that wouldn't be wise, snow and fire just don't mix."

"What do I have to lose?" The Snow Queen lowered her eyes as she unleashed a deadly blizzard in the room and aimed it at Damian.

As Damian became enraged his whole body turned to fire and he sent a wave of flames towards the Queen. They were dead locked. As she threw ice, he melted it. Neither had the ability to win and the destruction ripped away at the palace. Just before the walls were about to come down, they both stopped at the same time.

"I told you...you will never beat me my dear. And you will never have my mirror." He laughed as he waved a hand and the mirror disappeared into the depths of hell.

"I had to try. No hard feelings Damian."

"No feelings at all, Queeny. But be warned, if you ever try anything like this again, I will turn lose all the demons of hell onto you. And I guarantee you will not survive." Damian snapped his fingers and in an instant he disappeared.

Turning towards the servants who huddled scared in the corner, she shook her head. They had been disobedient to her and allowed this to happen. For that, they had to be punished. They were a group of warmhearted hard-working people, who did not ask for the life that the Snow Queen forced them into. They wanted their freedom, and one day hoped they would get it. On that day they did. Just not in the way they wanted.

As the Snow Queen turned to Valeman, she felt the bile in her stomach. She would make him suffer for all that he had been a part of. His fate however, would not be as easy as the others.

"This could have all been so easy, yet you turned our wedding into a massacre. I could kill you now…but if I did, you wouldn't learn anything. I want you to remember this day and all that happened, because you didn't want to marry me. Your fate will be worse than all the others; you will have to live with all of this. Oh and one other thing…live with this."

The Polar Bear King

She cast her spell as she walked from the room. Valeman fell to the floor. His fate was sealed.

Mullins

Chapter 11: The Snow Queen Rises / The Fate of the Polar Bear King

The Snow Queen climbed the steps of the entry hall slowly. A half smile covered her lips. If she could not marry Valeman, then no one would. She felt some level of satisfaction. As she climbed, the statues she had created caught her eye. She had grown fond of her latest Jorgen. He was a ruggedly handsome man, and an even more handsome ice figure.

"Pity I had to kill all the servants." She spoke as she climbed the steps. "I guess the cleanup, will be on me for a moment. Good thing I spared one to serve me."

In the dining room, Valeman lay on the floor. He was alive but barely. His head felt as if it were being ripped apart from the inside out. He struggled to stand but could not. His legs would not move; for a moment he thought he was paralyzed. A feeling of fear ran through him. He struggled to focus his eyes, but could not. He did not think he had been poisoned but he didn't remember. He wondered if death would come soon.

The hours passed and he managed to roll over onto his stomach. He was able to use his arms to push himself up. He reached to the table and pulled down a platter of pure silver. In it, he hoped to see his reflection. As he tipped the platter to its side, his heart sunk. He screamed out in terror as he saw his reflection.

The man was no longer there, he was the Polar Bear King once more. His screams rang out through the castle, until they were replaced with loud roars. He had become the product of the Snow Queen's revenge, she cast a spell to make him permanently change and be a bear for the rest of his life.

The Polar Bear King

As the Snow Queen leaned out of her balcony, she heard the cries from below. "Revenge is a dish…that is best served cold." She laughed at herself. "Next on the agenda, I want that mirror, and neither the devil nor my sisters will stop me."

Before the Story: Elaida's Road to the Snow Queen / Tale as Old as Time

Elaida watched as her parents sent away the young Prince Henry. She couldn't understand why they did not welcome him there. They had once been promised to each other. She had even grown to be fond of him. Now he was gone and she would be alone once again.

As the carriage pulled away Elaida flew down the wooden staircase that led to the entry hall. With every step she became more angered.

"Mother, I do not understand. Why did you make him leave? He was my only friend." Elaida's eyes began to fill with tears as she pleaded with her mother.

The Polar Bear King

"My dear, sometimes things cannot be as we plan them. When you two were promised, things were different. You are older now and the abilities you have acquired would not allow you to marry him or any other innocent person. Until you learn to control your power and your rage, it just isn't safe." Her mother explained.

"Father, please reconsider this. I can learn to control it, I know I can."

"I agree with your mother, it is too dangerous. Someone might get hurt or even worse, die at your hands."

Elaida turned away as her tears flowed down her cheeks. With every step, her rage grew. She was tired of having the things she wanted, taken away because of fear. She turned to her parents and clinched her fists. As she took a deep breath, her tears turned to ice.

"I am tired of everyone deciding what is best for me. Who are you to decide what is right or wrong. I am a goddess. And you are…powerless."

As Elaida focused her abilities, the castle shook. Her sisters, who were on the second level, came running, fearing the building was crumbling around them. They arrived in time to see the ice shards fly from Elaida's hands.

The girls screamed as they came from behind her. Their parents lay dead in front of them. Freya looked Elaida in the face and shook her head. "What have you done? How could you kill them?"

Elaida stepped down off the bottom step and walked over to the bodies of her parents. "They made him leave. They took away the last thing that kept me human. They said I was dangerous to others. Maybe they were right."

Coming Soon - *The Rise Of The Snow Queen Book Two: The War Of The Witches*

If you enjoyed this book, please go online and leave positive feedback.

About the Author

G.W. Mullins is an Author, Photographer, and Entrepreneur of Native American / Cherokee decent. He has been a published author for over 10 years. His writing has focused on the paranormal and Native American studies. Mullins has releases several books on the history/stories/fables of the Native American Indians.

Among his books are the extremely successful *The Native American Story Book - Stories Of The American Indians For Children Volumes 1-5*, *The Native American Cookbook*, and *Walking With Spirits Native American Myths, Legends, And Folklore Volumes 1 Thru 6*.

He has released books in his Sci/fi Fantasy Series *From The Dead Of Night* series, including the Best-Selling titles - *Daniel Is Waiting*, and *Daniel Returns*. In Fall of 2017 Mullins released a prequel to the *From The Dead Of Night* series titled *Daniel Awakens A Ghost Story Begins* which was a huge fan favorite and free gift to fans before the last installment *Daniel's Fate A Ghost Story Ends* is released in summer 2019. He did announce that Daniel would be returning in a second series in the coming years.

His most recent work includes the new series *Rise Of The Snow Queen* featuring Book One *The Polar Bear King*, and Book Two War Of The Witches. He also released *Messages from the Other Side* (a nonfiction book about communication with the dead), and the soon to be released *Convergence* (a post-apocalyptic book multi-series event coming in 2020).

For further information, on the writing, visit G.W. Mullins' web site at
http://gwmullins.wix.com/books

www.ingramcontent.com/pod-product-compliance
Lightning Source LLC
LaVergne TN
LVHW091556060526
838200LV00036B/864